Scout's Big Race

Story by Lori Mortensen
Illustrations by Nikki Boetger

One day, Scout and Flora went to soccer practice. The coach told everyone about a big race.

"The 'Fun Run Challenge' is a mile long," said the coach. "It will help you get fit for soccer."

"I raced in the 'Fun Run Challenge' last year," said Scout.

"You did?" said Flora. "A mile is a long way."

"I wore my favorite running shoes," said Scout, "but I only came in *fourth*."

"You need more than good shoes," said the coach. "You have to make healthy choices and get fit."

"What kinds of choices?" asked Scout.

"Eating healthy foods,

getting lots of sleep,

and exercising every day,"
the coach replied.

"I can make good choices," said Scout,
"and this time, I'll win the race."

"I'll help you!" said Flora.

After practice, Scout went to Flora's house for a snack. The smell of fudge brownies filled the air. Scout reached for one— then he remembered what the coach had told him.

"Let's eat something healthy," said Scout.

"Good idea," said Flora.

She took some oranges from the fruit bowl.

"Yum!" said Scout.

That night, Scout
went to bed early.

He was excited about the race.
He could *see* himself winning it.

*I just need to keep making
healthy choices,* he thought.

The next day, Scout and Flora met at the track. They saw that four laps around the track equaled one mile.

As Scout started running,
Flora waited to count each lap.

Running was easy at first, but after one lap, Scout slowed down.

Soon, he was hardly running at all.

"Keep going!" said Flora. "Only one lap to go!"

Scout kept going, even though it was hard. A mile was a long way!

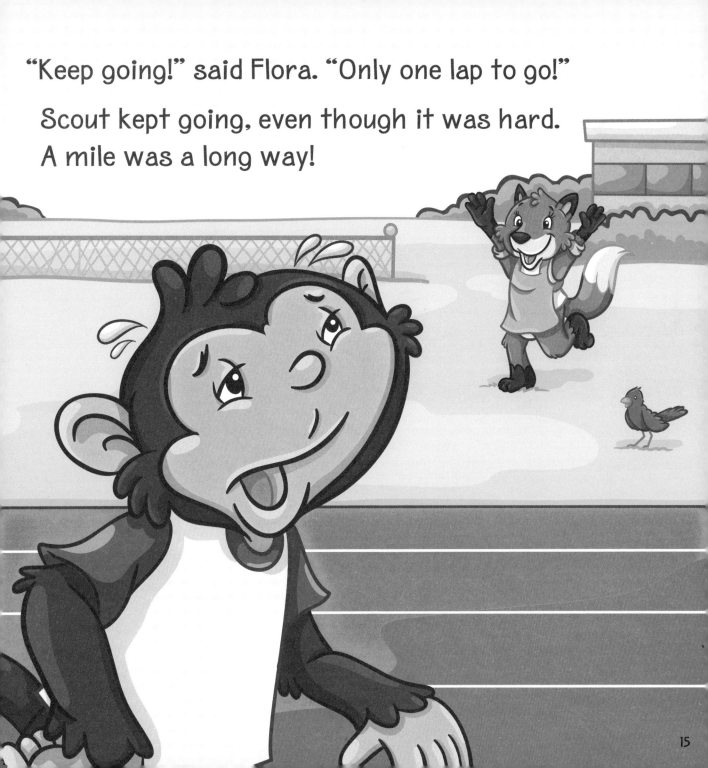

When Scout finished, he plopped down on a bench.

"Whew!" said Scout.

"Wow!" said Flora. "You ran a whole mile."

"I wasn't very fast this time," said Scout, "but if I keep running, I'll get faster."

Day by day, Scout kept
making healthy choices.
He ate fruits, vegetables,
and other healthy foods.

He got plenty of sleep.

And he ran every day.

"I know I can do it," said Scout.

Three weeks later, Scout and Flora
played in a soccer match.
Scout zipped back and forth
down the field with the ball.

"Wow!" said Flora. "You're faster than ever!"

"And I'm not even tired," said Scout.

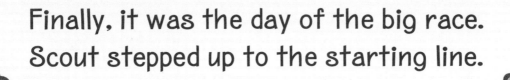

Finally, it was the day of the big race.
Scout stepped up to the starting line.

Today's the day! thought Scout.

"On your mark, get set ... GO!" yelled an official.

The runners took off.

As Scout raced around the track, other runners sprinted past him.

Uh-oh, thought Scout.
Am I going to be fourth again?

Scout ran by Flora.

"GO, SCOUT!" she cheered.

Scout grinned. He remembered how hard he had trained. He remembered racing faster and faster around the track.

It was time to do it again.

Scout pushed himself harder.
His legs pumped faster. One by one,
he slipped ahead of the other racers.

Scout rounded the last turn on his fourth lap.
Now, he could see the finish line.
His heart pounded in his chest.

I can win this, thought Scout . . .

Only 100 yards more . . .

Now just 50 yards to go.

Scout gave a final push,
swept past the last racer,
and flew across the finish line.

"I won!" said Scout. "I came in *first*!"

Scout had made a goal and trained hard.
Now he stood on the awards stand
with his first-place medal.

Making good choices felt terrific!

Glossary

fruits

run

vegetables

sleep